GENERAL STORE

GENERAL STORE

by Rachel Field
illustrated by Giles Laroche

 Little, Brown and Company
Boston · Toronto · London

Also illustrated by Giles Laroche
Sing a Song of People

Text for "General Store" is from the book
Taxis and Toadstools by Rachel Field.
Copyright 1926 by Rachel Field; renewed 1953
by Arthur S. Pederson. Reprinted by permission
of Doubleday and Company.

First edition

Library of Congress Cataloging-in-Publication Data

Field, Rachel, 1894–1942.
General store / by Rachel Field; illustrated by Giles Laroche. —
1st ed.
p.   cm.
Summary: A girl imagines the general store she will own someday
and all the things for sale in it, from bolts of calico to bunches
of bananas.
ISBN 0-316-28163-8 (lib. bdg.)
1. Children's poetry, American. [1. General stores — Poetry.
2. Stores, Retail — Poetry. 3. American poetry.]
I. Laroche, Giles, ill. II. Title.
PS3511.I25G401988b   87-37218
811'.52 — dc19   CIP
                                      AC

WOR

10 9 8 7 6 5 4 3 2 1

Published simultaneously in Canada
by Little, Brown & Company (Canada) Limited

Printed in the United States of America

To Claire and Romeo

— G.L.

Someday I'm going to have a store
With a tinkly bell hung over the door,

With real glass cases and counters wide

And drawers all spilly with things inside.

There'll be a little of everything:

Bolts of calico;

balls of string;

Jars of peppermint;

tins of tea;

Pots and kettles and crockery;

Seeds in packets;

scissors bright;

Kegs of sugar, brown and white;

Sarsaparilla for picnic lunches,

Bananas and rubber boots in bunches.

I'll fix the window and dust each shelf,

And take the money in all myself,

It will be my store and I will say:
"What can I do for you to-day?"